FREESTYLIN' AT THE FAIR

nickelodeon

THAT GIRL
Lay Lay

FREESTYLIN' AT THE FAIR

BY RHIANNON RICHARDSON

ILLUSTRATED BY DEANDRA HODGE

SCHOLASTIC INC.

ISBN 978-1-338-82499-5

10 9 8 7 6 5 4 3 2 1   23 24 25 26 27

Printed in the U.S.A.   40

First printing 2023

BOOK DESIGN BY SALENA MAHINA

TABLE OF CONTENTS

✦ CHAPTER 1 ✦

HARPER AND I WERE ON the edge of our seats. As Ms. Ortega's first class of the day, we would be the first to hear the decision about the upcoming Woodlawn Middle School Fair. After a week and four days of nonstop rain and thunderstorms, we would find out whether the fair would be indoors this year—for the first time *ever*.

Don't get me wrong—rain is important! I knew the flowers were going to be on point now that they'd had something to sip on. But I did not want the

fair to get rained out . . . or, I guess, rained in.
The fair is one of the best events of the year. Students
get to make the booths, and there's always a bomb
performance on opening night to kick off the
weekend.

This year, I'll be performing at the fair as That
Girl Lay Lay! I love that I can still be myself when
I walk the school halls, but I'd be lying if I said I
wasn't excited to show my friends and classmates
what I'm all about onstage. That's why this year has
to be perfect . . . and outside!

"How is she so calm?" Harper whispered. She
seemed just as anxious as I felt.

Harper and I had met up with our besties Akila,
Riley, and Giana at our lockers before coming to
class. Everyone was on edge, waiting to hear the fate
of the fair. No doubt our friends were currently
checking their phones every few seconds for our
promised update text.

"I don't know, but she's gonna have to spill soon
because I cannot take this," I huffed. I fanned myself
dramatically with my language arts homework. "For
once the bell for class to start can't ring soon enough."

Ms. Ortega was at her desk, reading and sipping on an iced coffee. When the bell finally rang, the room went quiet. Usually, Ms. Ortega gives us some time to finish talking and then she'll ring her gong to call our attention. But today, she froze with her mallet midair when she realized she already had all eyes on her.

"Well, good morning!"

She stood up and moved to the center of the room.

"How are we today, class?"

She looked at each of us, her rose-tinted smile warm and inviting.

"Honestly, I'm not doing so great, Ms. Ortega," someone said behind me.

I, along with everyone else, started to turn around. I caught Harper rolling her eyes and knew exactly who it was that had called out.

Terrell was slouched at his desk, limp and acting dramatic.

"Well, what's got you down, Terrell?" Ms. Ortega asked. She rested a hand on her hip.

Terrell sat up, folding his hands like he was about

to beg or pray. "Ms. Ortega, I am so *stressed*! I have *got* to know . . . Will the fair be inside or outside this year?"

We all snapped our attention back to the front of the room. For once, Terrell's goofiness was about to get us somewhere.

Ms. Ortega relaxed a little, and her smile grew three sizes.

"Well, Terrell, that *is* a good question—".

"Please tell us!" someone else called out.

That unleashed a wave of whining and pleading, giving Ms. Ortega an excuse to use her gong after all.

The gentle ring brought us all back to focus.

"Okay, okay. I'm not going to torture you any longer. I know how important the fair is to everyone. And as faculty chair of the student council, it's important to me, too. That's why I've decided that the fair will be . . . outside!"

"Whoooo!" I cheered along with the rest of the class. Harper and I high-fived, and when Sofia Montalvo held her hand out from the desk behind me, I high-fived her, too!

"Of course, we don't know what the weather will be like on the actual day," Ms. Ortega explained. "But after all that rain, the forecast for the coming days looks like clear skies. So it's safe to plan for the fair to be outdoors."

"This is gonna be great!" Sofia squealed.

"It is!" Ms. Ortega agreed. "It's especially important since we're hoping for a big turnout this year."

"Don't we want a big turnout every year?" Harper asked.

"Yes, but this year Woodlawn Middle School is donating all the proceeds from the fair to save the Woodlawn Food Bank," Ms. Ortega admitted, some of the excitement leaving her tone.

Even though everyone got a little caught up in the news, Ms. Ortega's words had my attention.

"Wait a minute. Why does the food bank have to be *saved*?" I asked.

"Oh, I know, I know!" Sofia's voice was practically in my ear as she leaned forward. I glanced back to see her arm raised, hand flapping in the air.

Ms. Ortega nodded at her to share with us.

"During the storms, a tree fell on the food bank. The whole roof caved in!"

A few people in class gasped.

"What?!"

"Oh my gosh!"

"Was anyone hurt?"

Ms. Ortega used her gong once more. Once we were quiet, she set the record straight and explained that the building had been closed. No one was inside when the tree fell. But the roof really *had* caved in, so the food bank had to move to a temporary space.

I tried to picture it: a whole tree falling on top of a building, crushing the roof. The thought gave me chills.

"They're operating out of Woodlawn Baptist Church until they can raise the money for repairs. With the fair right around the corner, the student council decided this would be the perfect cause to donate to," Ms. Ortega explained. "So all of you will be helping the food bank with your booths for the fair. And you can sign up to volunteer with the food bank as well. They could use the extra help right now, and the school has agreed to lead groups of students on Wednesday afternoons since those are early-release days."

I looked over to find Harper already looking at me. We nodded, silently agreeing to volunteer. We'd have to get Riley, Akila, and Giana on board, too. Now I was even more excited about the fair. Between me and my girls, I knew our booth was going to be amazing . . . whatever it turned out to be!

By third-period theater class, word had gotten around about the fair. As Akila and I made our way to Ms. Duncan's room after math class, I caught bits and pieces of conversations up and down the hall. Sofia was talking to another girl about a Broadway trivia game for their booth, and I overheard some of the kids from Giana's STEM club whispering about a ring toss game.

I couldn't wait to reunite with my girls so we

could get brainstorming. Akila and I slid into our seats at the same table as Giana, Riley, and Harper. I opened my mouth to speak, but I heard Riley's voice instead.

"You don't have to say it, Lay Lay," she said. "Harper already told us about signing up for volunteering—"

"Okay, but did you pick—"

"The same slot as you guys?" Giana asked. "Yes, girl, chill."

She laughed.

"Okay, okay," I said, throwing my hands up. "There's nothing wrong with making sure we're all on the same page. Speaking of which, we need to figure out what we're doing for our booth!"

"Lay Lay's right," Giana said. "We have two weeks before the fair."

"And I wanna win the secret competition," Akila added, twirling her pencil.

"What secret competition?" Riley asked as she pulled out her notebook.

"I think Reggie was talking about it in computer science," Giana said.

"Every year, there's a secret competition for the best booth," Akila explained. "Whichever booth collects the most tickets at the end is the winner."

"That has us written all over it," I said with full confidence. Between the five of us, we could bring any bomb idea to life.

"Lay Lay." Harper laughed a little. "We don't even know what we're doing yet. How do you know we're going to win?"

"Confidence is key," I told her, spitting straight facts. "I'm manifesting a fun booth that raises a lot of money and is so fire it's the best at the whole fair. No cap."

"I can hop on that," Akila said, backing me up.

"Me too!" Giana, Harper, and Riley agreed one by one.

Before we could all dive into a full-blown brainstorm, Ms. Duncan pulled our attention to her.

"I know with today's news about the fair that we're all excited and inspired," she said. "I love that energy! I promise you'll have time to work on your booths for the fair. I'll even give you time in

class to use some of the theater department materi-
als. But that time is *not* right now. Okay?"

She stopped at the front of the room and grabbed
a stack of worksheets. As Ms. Duncan passed out the
papers, it was clear that our brainstorm session was
officially on hold.

·✦·· CHAPTER 2 ··✦·.

I NEARLY TRIPPED OVER MY feet running to my locker. After theater class, I was more than ready for lunch. Clear skies meant lunch in the school courtyard! Plus, this would be a great chance for me and my girls to exchange ideas.

I traded my books for my lunch bag and nearly bumped into Giana after I closed my locker door.

"Slow down before you twist your ankle or something," she teased, laughing as she pushed her glasses up on her nose.

"I don't wanna waste any time," I said, falling in step beside her on our way to Riley, Akila, and Harper.

"Oh, I hope Akila brought her speaker," Giana said. "Then we could listen to the new Korey Vine album!"

"Girl, you're a real one! That would definitely level up lunchtime," I said. Korey's music was already playing in my head from memory.

Korey Vine was one of my favorite R&B artists. He had a great voice, was from Woodlawn, and he started his singing career when he was around my age! One of the cool things about following someone with a career as long as his was getting to see how much their sound had grown and changed over the years. And the fact that it'd been more than ten years blows my mind because he was still relevant and on point. That was one of the reasons my friends and I loved him. Heck, I'm pretty sure most of the kids at Woodlawn listened to his music, especially because he was from here. His latest album dropped this past weekend. But between recording and doing an interview for a local magazine, I still hadn't listened to the whole thing.

Giana and I wove between the current of students headed toward the cafeteria. Even though I usually buy lunch, when I saw the weather report on my phone last night for some long-overdue sunshine, I packed my lunch so I wouldn't have to wait in line. Maybe it was over the top, but I texted my girls, too, and told them to pack so we could go straight outside after theater class.

At their lockers, Harper and Akila were touching up their hair and makeup in Harper's locker mirror. Behind them, Riley pulled out her lunch box and an extra container, which meant she prepared treats! All the more reason to get outside ASAP for some sunshine and sweets.

Before she closed her locker, I snatched Akila's speaker, winking when she gave me a questioning look.

When we reached the end of the hall, Akila and I pushed both doors open at the same time. The warmth pressed against me like a hug, and we all had to stop and blink away the brightness.

"No more rain!" I breathed, opening my arms wide.

"Refreshing," Giana agreed. "Barely any clouds, too."

"Y'all are dramatic," Harper teased.

We followed the path that leads to the courtyard, which was flanked with plants and flowering bushes.

"Have you guys listened to *Lagoon Time* yet?" Giana asked.

"That album is dope," Akila said, shaking her head like she couldn't believe it. "Korey keeps getting better and better."

"I started listening to it," Riley said, repositioning her treat container on top of her lunch box.

"Do you need any help with that?" I asked.

"Help eating it or carrying it?" she asked, making all of us laugh. "It's okay, I got it. And we're almost there, anyway."

"I heard Korey is going to be in Woodlawn," Harper chimed in.

"For *real*? Where'd you hear that?" I asked.

Imagine if I ran into Korey Vine in the historic part of town. Maybe at the grocery store or when I was picking up a wrap at Mr. Paul's vegan cafe.

Korey seemed like a historic Woodlawn kind of guy. Someone who was into the culture and vibe . . . I'd recognize him, maybe he'd recognize me, we'd talk about music, and I'd boss my way into a feature on his next album . . . Ooooh, a girl could dream!

"I think I saw it online," Harper explained. "He gave an interview and mentioned heading home for a short break before the *Lagoon Time* tour."

"That would be so cool," Akila said. "What if he showed up at the fair?"

"Korey Vine is a grown man," Giana pointed out. "Why would he come to a middle school fair?"

That brought us down from cloud nine real fast.

"Well, you never know," Riley said slowly. "He did grow up in Woodlawn . . ."

"Okay y'all, if we really think Korey Vine might show up to the fair, then we *absolutely* need to start talking about ideas for our booth," I said. "We gotta show up *and* show out."

I knew the chances of a celebrity like Korey Vine coming to the fair were slim, but the idea was enough to get me excited all over again and ready to focus. The girls agreed, and as we rounded the corner of the school before the courtyard, the gears in my head started turning—

I stopped dead in my tracks when I saw what was ahead.

"I know that's not Terrell and his boys sitting at our tree." I shook my head. So much for those good vibes!

"Uh-uh, they need to move," Akila agreed.

"That's our spot!" Giana narrowed her eyes.

I couldn't even appreciate how the hydrangeas were blooming, or how the sun was at its peak, casting a yellow glow over everything. No, all I could see was Terrell, Reggie, and his boys sitting in our shady spot underneath our favorite oak tree.

Eating lunch in the courtyard was worth the hype because of this spot with this tree. It was a southern oak: not too big, filled out in all the right places with enough leaves to create the perfect patch of shade for me and my girls. It even had a few low branches for us to climb and sit on. When the weather got warm enough for us to eat outside, this was our spot. *Always.* And *everybody* knew that.

"Terrell. Reggie," I said, standing just outside the shade of our tree with my arms crossed.

"Lay Lay," Terrell matched my tone, and Reggie stood right behind him.

"Y'all need to move a little to the left because this is our spot," I said. "Always has been, is, and always will be."

"We got here first, though, so I guess it's ours today—"

"But you know we always sit here," Harper chimed in. "Why are you trying to act different?"

"Y'all really care *that* much about a tree?" Reggie asked.

"If you don't care, then why don't you move?" Giana asked, making a good point.

Terrell and Reggie looked at each other, raising their eyebrows in some kind of private conversation. When they looked at us again, I could already tell they were about to talk some noise.

"Why don't we just share? You sit over there, and we sit here."

I rolled my eyes and turned to see my girls shaking their heads, too.

"This is where the shade is," Riley said. Though her voice was quiet, she got straight to the point.

"Okay, okay, fine," Terrell said, holding up his hands. "How about we make a deal."

"A deal where you move over and give us our spot back?" Akila said. "Sure."

"More like a competition," Reggie clarified.

I looked around at my girls. Akila's eyes lit up with that competitive fire she brought to her gymnastics. And Giana's eyes pierced mine with a confidence I'd seen more and more recently.

Harper rolled her flawlessly rimmed eyes with slight annoyance, but her smile let me know she was game. And Riley's ginger ponytail bobbed as she gave me a silent nod. We had one another's backs and knew we could handle anything these boys were about to throw at us.

"What is it?" I asked.

"Well, you know the fair is coming up, and there's the secret booth competition," Reggie began.

"*We* propose a competition of our own, between us," Terrell interrupted Reggie, way too excited for this. "Whichever one of our booths earns the most tickets gets the tree."

"I'll shake on that." Giana spoke up first.

Riley, Akila, and I shook on it, too. Terrell, Reggie, and their friends against FiveStar. That was the name the five of us came up with when we performed together in the talent show a few months ago.

"We got this," I told my friends boldly.

"In the meantime, neither of us should get the tree," Giana pointed out.

"Nah, somebody else will take it," Terrell pointed out. "It's a bomb spot, for real."

"I think Giana's right, though," Reggie said. I honestly never thought I'd hear those words from him, but I kept quiet. "In the name of fair competition, how about we can't sit in the shade, but we can stay close to the tree so nobody steals it?"

We all agreed. The boys moved over and we picked a spot on the edge of the shade, too. Even though we were ready to get to work creating the best booth, we decided to wait until later. With the boys near us, we didn't want any eavesdropping!

·✦· CHAPTER 3 ·✦·

LATER THAT NIGHT, WE ALL hopped on a group
video chat to brainstorm fair booth ideas. There
was a lot at stake: helping the Woodlawn Food
Bank, winning the booth competition, and getting
our lunchtime spot back. Our booth had to be fire
and then some.

"Hey, guys!" Riley's smiling face lit up my screen
first.

"Hey!" Akila hopped on. She was putting her
braids up in her silk bonnet for the night.

"One sec," Harper said, setting down her phone to take one more swipe up her cheeks and down her jaw before putting away her jade roller. She said it was the *key to her complexion* since it helped all her serums and creams sink in.

"Let me put my glasses on." Giana let out a yawn, already tucked in and looking cozy with her bright blue comforter pulled up to her shoulders.

"So, I don't know about everyone else, but I have an idea for a booth!" I jumped in right away.

The thought popped into my head when Tasha picked me up from school and one of my favorite songs was playing on the radio in the car.

"Already?" Akila said. "Okay, Lay Lay, the floor is yours."

"Well, we already dominated the talent show a few months ago. So, the obvious way to win *again* is to power up as FiveStar, as a girl group that sings, dances, and raps."

"Huh . . . I don't know . . ." Riley said slowly.

"Yeah, Lay, I feel like the booth has to be an activity for the people who come to the fair, not something for *us* to do," Harper added, not a single strand of hair out of place as she tilted her head to the side under her lamplight.

"Well, we don't have to be the ones singing," Giana pointed out. "Lay Lay is right. FiveStar didn't just sing, we created a vibe. What if we bring that same energy but have the fair-goers be the performers? Like a karaoke booth?"

"Yesss, girl!" I squealed. "Exactly."

Giana's smile got wider. We were on the same wavelength!

Looking at my screen, I realized Giana's was the only smiling face looking back at me.

"Karaoke is a great idea," Riley admitted. But her words didn't match up with her scrunched brow. "It's just that when we sang in the talent show, we were there to compete. The fair isn't *actually* a competition. This isn't about us being better than Terrell or Reggie or beating our classmates. We have to make a booth that's best for the fair."

"Yeah," Akila chimed in. "And, like Riley said, karaoke is a great idea . . . It just might not be the *best* idea."

"We have to be strategic and do what's best

for the food bank, too," Harper added.

"What's best for the food bank is for us to band together, use our combined strength to make a bomb idea come to life, and raise the most money possible," I reminded them. I wondered what was not clicking.

"Okay, but music is *your* strength, Lay Lay," Harper pointed out.

"True," I agreed. "But, like Giana said, we wouldn't even be singing that much. It's about creating a fun experience for the people who come to the fair. We might do a few numbers here and there to get people hyped up—"

"But that's just it, Lay Lay," Akila interrupted. "Not all of us *want* to be singers . . ."

Harper and Riley nodded in agreement.

I sighed. I had jumped on the call pumped and ready for us to come together, but now I didn't know what to think.

"Well, what do you guys want to do for a booth?" Giana said sleepily as she slipped into another yawn. "We're supposed to be brainstorming, so let's see what else we can come up with."

I saw Akila open her mouth, but Riley cleared her throat.

"I mean, I had this idea for a pie baking contest," she began. "I wouldn't be the judge—anyone who tries some pie would get to vote. I feel like that's a classic fair thing. People can compete, and . . . well, you know, people gotta eat."

She had me there. One of my favorite things about going to the fair was the food. Local restaurants set up booths to sell their one-of-a-kind snacks, and food trucks pulled up in the parking lot and set up picnic tables. Playing all the games and walking around from booth to booth always had me working up an appetite.

I knew Riley's pie booth would be an exceptional addition to the culinary kings and queens, especially if she entered a pie. Woodlawn would be lucky to taste her treats!

"I guess if we're putting stuff out there, Akila and I had an idea, too," Harper added. "We thought it would be cool to have a tie-dye booth—"

"I could teach people about batik," Akila chimed in. "It's a Nigerian dyeing technique."

"What did you originally say about it, Akila?" Harper asked.

"A classic with a cultural twist," she said, rolling her wrist and snapping on twist.

"That's a great idea," Giana admitted.

Four sets of eyes darted around my screen, looking everywhere and at me at the same time. I could tell we were all wondering the same thing: *Which idea do we use?*

All the ideas were good ones. But I knew the best way I could help at the fair and make money for the food bank was with music. And the best way for my girls to help out was by using their strengths . . .

"Y'all are right," I said, starting to get hyped again. "We each have our own things. Music is mine. Riley is a great baker, and she should show off her talents! And Akila and Harper, you're both artists. Tie-dye is a classic, and people will line up for it. Plus, adding that touch of your culture will make it so cool."

"And the karaoke booth will be the perfect place for me to test a light show program I've been coding on my Bluetooth speaker," Giana chimed in.

"The lights change color with the beat. We could have a light show going while people sing."

"Slow that roll, sis," I said. "You *coded* your speaker to *change color* on *beat?*"

When she nodded, my head flooded with a million questions. *How? When? Why is this the first we're hearing about it?*

"Gi, show us!" I squealed. "That sounds so cool."

"Yeah, I wanna see," Harper added eagerly.

"Go on, put on a show right now!" I said. "Show us what you got."

A little pink flushed Giana's cheeks, but she got out of bed to turn off her lights and propped her phone up so we could see the speaker. When she turned it on, a ring light around the edge of the cube lit up and was the only thing we could see in the dark.

She put on one of our favorite '90s songs, "Real Love," recorded by Mary J. Blige. The light changed from pink to blue to green to purple. As the beat picked up, the light changed faster. As the beat slowed, the changes were smoother. It was dope, and I just had to sing along.

Soon, we were all singing and shimmying to the rhythm. I couldn't help but laugh when Harper held up her hairbrush like a mic and spun around with her phone in her hand.

"You're gonna make me dizzy," Akila said, giggling.

Giana turned the light back on when the song ended, and we started talking over one another telling her how cool the speaker was.

"So, it's settled," I said. "We have three great ideas, and they all deserve a booth at the fair. Ain't nothing wrong with that."

"So . . . We're not picking just one?" Riley asked.

"Why pick one when we can do it all?" Harper said, making everyone smile.

"So, Lay and Giana, Harper and Akila, and . . . me."

"But wait, what about the booth competition?"

Akila's question made the reality of our decision settle in. If we weren't working with one another, then we were against one another for the secret competition. As far as Terrell and Reggie went, I figured Giana and I would just have to pull through and beat them on our own with our karaoke booth.

"A little bit of friendly competition never hurt anyone," Harper said with a shrug, though the way her voice tapered off left me feeling unconvinced.

·✦· CHAPTER 4 ·✦·

"SO, WE'RE GOING TO DO three booths instead of one," I told my cousin Tasha as we grabbed our smoothies from the drive-through window. "That way all of us get to do what we do best."

Tasha thanked the barista before pulling out and turning toward my school. When my parents were out of town, she gave me a ride, and we almost always stopped for smoothies.

"I think that's a good idea," Tasha said, holding out her Blueberry Boom to me. I tapped my Mango

31

Masterpiece against it, toasting to a good morning and to us getting out of the house on time. I sipped my drink and took a second to collect my thoughts. Even though I was glad we'd come up with good ideas, I'd be lying if I said I wasn't a little down about not working with all four of my friends.

Tasha seemed to sense my doubts. "You know, it doesn't take five people to run *one* booth at a fair," she pointed out. "You and your friends are still working together for the fair, just in your own ways."

She was right, and thinking about it that way definitely helped.

"And it's what's best for the food bank," I replied, remembering what Harper had said last night.

"I still can't believe a *tree* fell on the roof," Tasha said, shaking her head. "I'm just glad no one was hurt."

"Ms. Ortega said they might have to close the food bank altogether."

"Yeah, I heard that, too," Tasha replied. "Though it wouldn't disappear. If the Woodlawn Food Bank can't afford the repairs, they might have to close and become part of a larger food bank in a town nearby."

"Then there'd be no food bank in Woodlawn," I said. "That means the fair has to be everything and then some!"

"You know, if Giana wants, there are some old speakers and mics laying around where I work at the Hayes Theater. We recently got new equipment. I can ask my boss if you guys can borrow some of the old stuff so Giana can geek out."

"Really?!" I was practically falling out of my seat. The equipment at Hayes—even the old stuff—is made for professional performing. That would take our karaoke booth to the next level!

"Yeah, girl! I'll ask my boss about it today."

"Well, thank you!" I was so excited and I hadn't even finished my smoothie yet.

When I walked into language arts, Ms. Ortega was handing out stacks of flyers to a group of us who had volunteered to put them up around school. Luckily, Harper, Riley, Giana, and Akila had also volunteered. I would get to spend time with my friends during school for once!

"Remember, you have a half hour," Ms. Ortega said. "Then you're all due back to your first-period class. I don't want to get calls from teachers saying you were late or messing around in the hallway, okay?"

I caught Giana's eye and she grinned back at me. I hadn't told her yet about Tasha hooking us up with equipment for our karaoke booth.

"Oh, Lay Lay, look at this." Akila held out one of the flyers. I glanced at the paper and saw the usual info: the dates and time of the fair, and the field where it would be held. But then the text at the bottom caught my eye:

INCLUDING A SPECIAL OPENING NIGHT PERFORMANCE BY WOODLAWN'S OWN ALAYA HIGH (THAT GIRL LAY LAY)!

The student council member who had designed the flyers had even used a cool graffiti font for my mention! I loved it.

"I still can't believe it," I admitted to my friends. "I'm gonna perform at the fair I've been going to every year since I was a little kid."

"It's so cool," Giana agreed. "It shows you how far you've come."

"I can't wait," Akila said. "It's been a minute since I've seen you live on a stage and not just free-stylin' online."

Ms. Ortega dismissed us with another warning to be back on time. In the hallway, pairs started breaking off to go in different directions.

"Lay Lay, let's go this way," Giana said. She took a few steps toward the science hall. "Maybe we can stop in the computer science room and I can show you the code for the speakers."

"Good idea," I said, already following her.

"Where are you guys going?" Harper asked, some playful *excuse me* sass in her voice.

"We're going to put up flyers in the science hallway while we talk about our karaoke booth."

"That's actually a good idea," Akila admitted, looking from me and Giana to Harper. "This would be a great chance for us to swing by the art wing and see if Mr. Glazer can help us with our booth."

Akila and Harper paired off, already murmuring about dye colors.

"Oh . . . uh—okay," Riley muttered, more to herself than to me and Giana. She looked a little lost as she watched Akila and Harper disappear around the corner. It didn't feel right to leave her on her own. But I wasn't sure how productive we could all be when we weren't working on the same project.

"You gonna be okay, Riles?" I asked.

"You could take the hallway by the cafeteria to cover more ground," Giana offered before I could just tell her to come with us.

"That's a—uh—good idea, Giana," Riley said quickly. "Thanks." And with that, she headed in the opposite direction, alone.

"Come on, Lay. Let's talk shop."

I shook off any discomfort I felt at watching Riley go off on her own.

"So, you're in charge of all the technical stuff, Gi," I said. "I hope you know that."

"Yup, and you're in charge of the design stuff," she countered.

"Perfect!"

"So, have you thought about what the booth should look like?"

"Dim lighting, a platform, a screen to display the lyrics," I rattled off. I made a mental note to ask Tasha if they'd have that kind of thing at the Hayes.

We paused to hang a few flyers around the water fountain.

"Speakers, TV, mics—"

"Light strips for the speakers," Giana added.

"We could go to the craft store and pick out a cool fabric as the backdrop for the stage—"

"We could make it look like a concert!" Giana said, gripping her stack of flyers with full excited force.

The second she said "concert," I could see the booth in my imagination.

We continued hanging posters and stopped in the computer science classroom so Giana could show me her code. I didn't understand all the symbols and sequences, but Giana explained that she's refining the program to track beats better and change color according to the tempo. I can't wait to see the updates in action.

We took the long way back to Ms. Ortega's room, looking for areas our classmates hadn't covered. Suddenly the door to the boys' bathroom swung open and almost hit me.

"Whoa!" I said, jumping back just in time.

"Yo, I didn't see you." Terrell stepped into the hallway. "My bad, my bad . . . Hey, Giana."

"Hi, Terrell," Giana said, glancing at her watch.

I caught her drift, knowing Ms. Ortega was serious about us making it back on time. Giana and I got on our way.

"Hey, Lay Lay," Terrell called out.

We stopped and turned back. Terrell was looking at one of the fair flyers on the wall.

"Congrats on performing at the fair," he said, gesturing at the flyer. "That'll be pretty cool, seeing you up there."

"You gonna watch me perform?" I asked, trying to hide my surprise.

"I mean—uh—I'm gonna be at the fair, anyway, like, at my booth and stuff. So, why not?" I could tell he was trying to play it off, but I appreciated it.

Like Giana said before, Terrell giving me props was another reminder of how far I've come. It's still weird to think of Terrell as someone other than that boy who used to tease me in elementary school. But if I can grow and my girls can grow, I guess Terrell can grow a little, too.

"Thanks, I'm excited for it," I said. "Performing for my friends and classmates will be cool."

He left it at that, and Giana and I booked it back to Ms. Ortega's room for the rest of first period.

·✦· CHAPTER 5 ·✦·

IN HONOR OF OUR TRUCE with the boys, we picked a spot close to the tree but not in the shade for lunch. Even though the sun was beating down, the grass was soft and I'd been looking forward to my poke bowl all morning.

I helped Riley spread out the picnic blanket she brought for us to sit on.

"Were you guys able to figure out what you need for your booths?" I asked as I speared a piece of ahi tuna with my fork.

"I think so," Harper admitted. She looked to Akila for confirmation.

"Yeah, we went to the art wing this morning and Mr. Glazer gave us some advice on simple designs that we can teach at our booth," Akila explained.

"Oh, and he's going to help us mix dye so we can have unique colors instead of what you buy in a store," Harper added as she unwrapped her sandwich. "I'm excited to see what we come up with!"

I eyed Harper's delicious looking lunch.

"Is that a veggie banh mi?" I asked. I was hoping for a bite—the toasted mini baguette looked so good! Harper's mom, Ms. Pham, is always on point with her Vietnamese specialties. Something about pickled veggies hits the spot and takes the flavor game to the next level.

Harper smiled as she peeled back the foil to reveal the sliced-off end of the baguette. It's her least favorite part of the bread, and my favorite!

"My mom remembered to cut off the end this time."

"Thank youuuuuu!" I gushed, thankful for the clean edge. Harper and I have had disastrous results in the past trying to tear it off or cut it with a plastic knife from the cafeteria.

"Tasha is getting us some sound equipment from Hayes to use in our karaoke booth," Giana told everyone. "I'm gonna program it like I did my speaker."

"That's gonna be so cool," Akila said around bites of her turkey sub.

"What about you, Riley?" I asked, noticing she was a little quiet. She had another container with her today. Yesterday, her vegan cream puffs definitely helped us mellow out a little after our face-off with Terrell and Reggie.

"I made some of my own flyers to get the word out about my pie baking contest," Riley said. "And since I won't be judging, I started thinking of recipes I might try for the pie I enter. Oh, and I ran into Brendon and we hung up flyers together."

"Brendon *Evans*?" Harper asked as she leaned back in surprise.

Brendon Evans was another one of Terrell and Reggie's friends. He was in theater class with us and sat with the guys at lunch. He was the last person I'd expect Riley to link up with for *anything*.

"Yeah . . . It's not like I had anyone else to do it with . . ."

The weird feeling I got before when we left Riley by herself came back now. So it *had* bothered her. I guess I wasn't surprised. It probably would've bothered me, too.

"What's in the container, Riles?" Akila asked.

Riley jumped and glanced down at the container in her lap like she had forgotten it was there. "Oh, I made these mini puff pastries. The dough is too flaky, but I might use this filling for my pie. Wanna taste?"

"Do *we?*" I said. I nearly rolled over when she popped the lid and a sweet, warm, peachy aroma wafted out.

We fell silent—this time without the awkward tension—as we all savored the silky sweetness of Riley's peach pastries.

"I figure I can test out recipes and the samples can be fun snacks for us these next two weeks," Riley admitted. She sat back and watched our faces for our reactions.

"Mmmm mmm mmmmm, delicious," I said through my second bite.

"I say this is an eleven out of ten," Harper chimed in, eyes still closed in bliss.

"One hundred out of ten, period!" Giana swooned.

A breeze blew by, and a second later a thud caught us off guard. A wayward basketball rolled to a stop in the grass a few feet away.

"Pass it back," Terrell shouted through cupped hands, acting like he was far away even though he and his friends were sitting too close for comfort.

I rolled my eyes but got up and grabbed the ball.

"Try to keep this over there," I said as I handed it back to Terrell.

"Soon this won't be an issue anymore, when you have to sit somewhere else—"

"Aht aht." I stopped him, holding up a hand. "You mean when y'all have to sit somewhere else. It's you who's gonna have to move, because my girls and I got this in the bag!"

"You seem so sure—"

"It's called confidence, Terrell," I said, ready to talk a little noise.

"Right, you got confidence in you *and* ya girls. But word is you and ya girls aren't working together."

"Where'd you hear that?" I asked.

Even though it was true, we hadn't gone around telling people we split up for the fair . . . at least not yet.

"Well, I heard Akila talking to Mr. Glazer about supplies for a tie-dye booth," Reggie said, joining the conversation with Brendon right behind him.

"And Riley told me about her pie Bake-Off booth while we were hanging flyers," Brendon said. "I might enter my grandma's apple pie."

"And in free period, Giana was coding on one of the computers," Terrell added. "When Oscar Tomlinson asked what she was doing, she said something about programming a karaoke speaker."

"Okay, and . . . ?" I kept my cool, though finding out they knew so much about our plans when I knew nothing about theirs threw me a little.

"I'm just surprised," Reggie said. He shook his head. "If you're not working together, you're working against one another. They're your competition for the best booth. No secrets means no edge."

"I don't need an *edge* when it comes to my girls," I said. "I trust them. If you can't trust your boys, maybe you need new friends."

Terrell looked at Reggie and Brendon. Reggie just shrugged. "I'm just saying, if we weren't all working together, I wouldn't just be putting my brilliance out there for the taking."

"Nobody is trying to take your 'brilliance,' Reggie, trust me," I said, laughing a little.

"She's got you there, 'cause I'm the brains here," Terrell teased. He tossed the basketball to Reggie fast, like he wanted to catch him off guard.

I headed back over to my girls. Harper was showing Giana a new eyeliner technique and Akila was sampling her second pastry from Riley's container. I sat back down, but my mind wasn't completely there with my friends anymore.

I knew I could trust my girls. That was an absolute fact. We didn't play dirty, not together and not against one another. But the reason we weren't working together in the first place was because we couldn't agree on the best booth idea. And only the best idea could win.

·✦· CHAPTER 6 ·✦·

"DO YOU THINK THIS WILL be enough?" a voice asked from behind a box overfilled with speakers, wires, and other technical equipment.

"How'd you make it up here if you can't see?" I laughed a little as I got up from my seat to help Tasha with the box.

"Pure memory and excellent spatial awareness," she replied.

I looked through the box. She managed to fit

four speakers in with the mics, wires, stands, and a power strip.

"This should work, but I think it's ultimately up to Giana," I admitted. "She's the technical one."

Then I noticed a string of purple feathers in the box.

"Wait, what's this?" I asked.

"I found some old costume stuff that you guys can borrow, too," Tasha replied. "I think there are a few hats, some feathers, and some glasses. I figured people can dress up and sing."

"Thanks, Tasha! This is perfect."

"Good," Tasha said. "Well, I'm gonna log out and then I can give you a ride on my way home, okay?"

I packed up my homework and waited while Tasha locked up her office. We put a couple of the speakers in a second box so neither of us would have to carry anything too heavy to the car.

"Do we pass the food bank on the way?" I asked once we were buckled in.

Tasha thought about it for a second. "Sure, we can head that way if you want."

"Yes, please."

We cut through historic Woodlawn, a district full of red-brick buildings with colorful awnings and painted windows showcasing a variety of store-fronts. Mr. Paul's was my favorite vegan cafe, and the mystic shop on the corner had some of the most beautiful crystals I'd ever seen.

When the Woodlawn Food Bank came into view, it was at the end of a U-shaped driveway that was blocked off with cones and caution tape.

"Whoa." I couldn't help myself. My jaw dropped as we slowed down to take in the sight.

Even though the tree that had hit the building had been cleared away, the entire roof was caved in and the side of the building had been crushed. We could even see the different floors and some of the office furniture on the upper levels. When we pulled away, I caught a glimpse at the stump that remained. I couldn't believe a tree so big could really fall . . .

It made me think of our tree in the courtyard at school. It wasn't as big as the one here used to be, but it had always felt big to us. I could see a branch or two falling off in a storm, but the tree trunk cracking down the middle felt impossible—that was, until now.

Tasha was speechless, too. The excitement over getting the equipment for my booth dissipated. All I could think was: *Was the fair really going to be enough to fix that?*

Wednesdays were early-release days. Most of the time, I liked to do some kind of self-care as a midweek reset. Sometimes this meant a face mask and deep condition at home while I watched *The Charlene Wilson Show*, and other times it meant quality time with my girls as we got our nails done.

This week, we had booked manicures at Selma's Salon at the Woodlawn Walk. It's an awesome outdoor mall with stores that sold things from all over the world. It would be the perfect place to find cool decor for our booths.

Jordyn was Selma's daughter. She was my favorite

nail tech because she knew how to do detailed designs. All five of us got stars on our nails in honor of FiveStar. Our base colors were different, but we each compared the designs while we were sitting side by side for our pedicures.

"So, what else is new, girl?" Jordyn asked me when she brought over some sparkling waters.

"We're getting ready for the Woodlawn Middle School Fair next week," I told her as I sipped on some bubbles. "I'll be back to get my nails done for my performance."

"I already have you on the books for next week," Jordyn said. She smiled so her dimples showed.

"You should come!" I told her. "It's gonna be great this year. We all have booths."

I gestured to my friends.

"Oh, nice!" Jorydn said. "I'll be there. My mom, too."

"Would you maybe put this up in the salon window?" Riley asked. She pulled a flyer out of her purse and handed it to Jordyn.

"We want to get the word out," Riley explained. "This year, the fair is raising money for the Woodlawn

Food Bank. The building was badly damaged by a big storm."

Jordyn smoothed the paper over her leg. "I'll put it up at the register," she said. "If you can get me more, I'll put some up around the salon so no one will miss it."

"We can definitely get you more," Riley said. She smiled and relaxed back into her seat.

"So, what are you guys doing for your booths?" Jordyn asked as she retwisted one of her bantu knots.

"Giana and I are making a karaoke booth," I said.

"Harper and I are doing tie-dye and batik," Akila said. "We're going to teach people about Nigerian culture, and they'll get to dye something to take home."

"That sounds fire!" Jordyn said, looking between us. "I mean, they both do."

She turned to Riley.

"And what about you, hon?"

"I'm hosting a pie Bake-Off," Riley said. "Anyone can enter their pie, and people at the fair can taste them and vote."

"You working all by yourself?" Jordyn asked. She glanced at all of us. I couldn't tell if she was trying to throw shade or genuinely asking.

"My parents are helping me," Riley said softly.

Jordyn nodded along, her smile growing. "Look at all you hardworking, innovative women coming through for your community. I love this!"

"We're hoping the fair raises enough money," Harper said. "If it doesn't, the food bank will have to dissolve."

"I wonder how expensive the repairs will be," Akila said. "Like, how much do you think we should be hoping to make?"

"I don't really know," Harper replied. "My mom said the damage was pretty bad. But we don't have any control over that. Let's focus on making the best booths we can."

We all agreed, but I couldn't help but wonder if Akila was on to something. My detour with Tasha flashed in my mind. The damage looked super expensive. What if the fair wasn't enough? What more could we do?

·✦· CHAPTER 7 ·✦·

WITH MY FINGERS SPARKLING AND my toes all glammed up, I was excited for a little Woodlawn Walk shopping. We picked a direction and started walking. In addition to the storefronts, smaller kiosks with cool, unique stuff lined the main walkway.

We passed a chocolate stand, a beautiful flower kiosk, and a crepe stand with a line so long we had to find a spot to cut through.

"Look at this!" Akila said as she charged toward a kiosk decked out with vibrant reds, yellows, and browns. It was filled with Hindu statuettes of elephants, colorful beaded jewelry, and books of henna designs. I passed incense and caught sharp scents of patchouli and sage. It smelled amazing!

We didn't end up buying anything, but as we walked away, Akila turned to Harper.

"I feel like the Indian music completed the vibe there, you know?"

"Yeah, you're right," Harper replied.

"Maybe I can make a mix of Nigerian music to play at our batik booth."

"That's a great idea," Harper agreed.

"Why would you guys play music at your booth when that's Lay Lay and my thing?" Giana asked. "I thought the whole point of us doing this separately is that you wanted your booth to *not* be music-related."

"We didn't say we want *no* music at our booth," Akila said, "and I doubt you guys are going to be the only booth that has music at the *whole* fair."

Akila turned back to Harper, and I caught Giana's eye. I gave a slight shrug for only her to see. Even though music was supposed to be our thing, I wasn't worried. We were picking mainstream music. Their music wouldn't copy ours . . . At least, it shouldn't.

I changed the topic and we started talking about what other kids were doing for their booths.

"Oscar Tomlinson is running a dunk tank," Harper said.

"Two girls in my art class are doing a face-painting booth," Akila said.

"Some kids in my STEM club are making a glow-in-the-dark ring toss game," Giana offered.

"What about Terrell and Reggie?" Harper asked. "Does anyone know what they're up to?"

"Yeah, they're the ones we really need to worry about if we want to get our tree back," Akila said matter-of-factly.

"They've had that basketball at lunch every day this week," I said, realizing the pattern suddenly. "I'm guessing they'll have some kind of basketball booth."

"Not surprised, and not worried," Harper said. She held out her hand for a high five.

"Riley, have you heard—"

We stopped walking and realized we were missing a redhead.

"Over there," Giana said. She pointed to Riley standing in front of a shop window a few doors down.

"Girl, you cannot step away like that," I said once we were closer. "We don't want to lose you."

"Sorry," Riley said quickly. "I just wanted to get a closer look at this."

She gestured toward Reading & Records, a music and bookstore. In the window a few records were propped up next to a purple record player. It was the Carpenters and Chaka Khan, an odd combination but definitely one I could rock with. The backdrop for the setup was a big orange-and-red tapestry with an abstract geometric pattern. There was something dizzying but cool about it.

"Come on," Riley said before I had a chance to ask what exactly she was looking at.

We followed her inside. The AC in the small store was refreshing, and the layout was pretty simple: books to the left, records to the right. Riley went straight to the window. She gently took the bottom edge of the tapestry between her fingertips.

"What do you think?" she asked, turning to us.

"About the . . . tapestry?" Harper said slowly, not

doing a good job at hiding her confusion *and* her answer.

"Yeah," Riley said, not picking up on the shade. "I think it would be the perfect pop of color for my booth. I could use it as a tablecloth."

She bent down to a small basket full of folded and wrapped tapestries. "And they're on sale!"

"Don't you think it's a little like what we'll have at our booth?" Harper asked. She stepped in for a closer look.

Riley found the tapestry from the display in the basket and stood up straight again. "I don't think so. You guys are doing tie-dye and batik. This is just a tapestry. Plus, I'm using it as a tablecloth."

"But look at the pattern," Harper pressed. "That's something we could teach people to make at our booth. The cloth looks like it *belongs* at our booth."

I looked to Akila, waiting for her to jump in and say it wasn't a big deal, but she just stood with her lips sealed and her arms folded.

"You guys are dyeing fabrics with traditional Nigerian patterns and giving lessons," Riley replied. "This is just a tablecloth, something you'd find at a picnic. Plus, it's going to be covered with pies."

Instead of leaving an opening, Riley headed for the cash register.

"I'm gonna buy it," she said over her shoulder. "Be right back."

The way she shut down that conversation was a little cold, but I understood. Harper's pressing wasn't going to change Riley's mind . . . even if Harper had a bit of a point.

"I'm gonna wait outside. It's cold in here," Harper said abruptly. Then she stepped out with Akila right behind her.

"Was that weird, or was that weird?" I asked, quiet enough so only Giana could hear.

"I don't think it's that big a deal," Giana said. "Akila showed us what they're gonna teach at their booth and I don't think the tablecloth looks anything like it . . ."

The way she trailed off left me unconvinced.

"What is it?"

"Not to be *that* person, but if they're going to play music at their booth, then Riley can have a tablecloth at hers."

I let it drop since Riley was back and we had to catch up with Akila and Harper. The *if they do this, then she can do that* felt a little sticky to me. We should all be doing whatever worked best in each booth rather than trying to one-up one another or get even.

"I'm hungry," I said, figuring the food court was neutral territory. "Y'all ready for lunch?"

I was feeling parched. We headed to the food court, and I gladly took a smoothie sample at the entrance. The sample guy started telling me how it's a cross between a smoothie and juice, with a smoother texture and just a little thickness. I took a sip and tasted the perfect collab between a tart berry and a sweet tropical *something*.

"This is *really* good," I said as I leaned in to read his name tag. "Jason."

"Thank you, I—uh—actually came up with the recipe."

Akila was right behind me, so I handed her a sample and then passed some to my other friends. "Y'all *gotta* try this!"

Soon, we were all sipping on what Jason called Bahama Berry.

"Giana, we _have_ to have this at our booth," I said, excited. "When people get done singing, they'll want something to drink. And _this_ is perfect."

Giana tossed her cup in the trash. "That's a great idea, Lay—"

"Okay, wait a second," Riley interrupted. "Why would you sell juice at your booth when my booth is food and drinks?"

"It's actually not a juice . . . it's—"

Akila shook her head at Jason, and he quietly stepped back to mind his business.

"It's just one drink, so if people need something after they sing it's right there," I explained.

"Plus, your booth is pie—" Giana started.

"And I said I was going to serve drinks, too. Why not just send people down to my booth if they're thirsty?" Riley asked.

I opened my mouth to respond, but then I stopped myself. Riley was right. If people got thirsty at our booth, the right thing to do would be to send them down to hers. We'd get traffic for the karaoke, and she'd get traffic, too. But why send them her way when Giana and I could build a better crowd at our booth? We were competing after all . . .

"So, we can't have a drink at our booth, but you can have a tapestry at yours?" Giana asked Riley. Then she turned to Akila and Harper. "And you guys can have music?"

"The music isn't the same." Harper stepped up to defense. "You guys are definitely not going to be the only booth with music, and you're playing mainstream music. We're going to play Nigerian music." She was making the same point she'd made before, but her head bob and attitude hit me the wrong way.

"No one is saying you can't do anything," Riley jumped in, her tone clipped. "I'm just pointing out that it's sus—"

"Since when do you say 'sus'?" Akila asked.

"Since she started acting like it with that 'tablecloth,'" Harper said. The words just spilled out. The second she said it, Harper's face went two shades paler. "I didn't mean—"

"I'm just looking out for myself," Riley snapped, her face flushed. "I don't have someone to run ideas by. I saw the tapestry and thought it would look good in my booth, so it's going in my booth. Period. If we wanted to have opinions on what everyone else is doing, we could've worked together."

I think all of us were a little shocked. There was a reason Riley's nickname was Smiley Riley. None of us knew what to say or do.

"Riley—" I started.

"No. You know what, I'm not hungry anymore. I'm just gonna call my dad and go home."

"Riles, no. Don't go, we should talk about this," I said, hating the distance I felt between us.

"Maybe we should, but I don't want to right now," she said, texting her dad. "My dad will be here soon. I'll see you guys in school tomorrow."

She didn't wait for us to argue. Watching her break away from the group was like watching a branch break off in a storm.

"Should we go after her?" Harper asked.

"I don't think so," I said, ready to call it a day, too. "See you all tomorrow?"

Akila and Harper mumbled good-byes, and Giana and I did the same. It was an awkward end to an uncomfortable afternoon.

·✦· CHAPTER 8 ·✦·

LATER THAT EVENING, I SAT on the family room carpet in front of Tasha and handed her my comb and hair oil. My parents were away for work, so she was staying with me for a few days. Tasha parted my hair, pulled off the first section, and finger combed warm oil through my natural coils and along my scalp. I found a cute movie and turned it on with the volume down. I leaned back against the front of the armchair Tasha was sitting in and closed my eyes.

As fun as it was to go to the salon and try out new hairstyles, there was something simple and relaxing about having Tasha braid my natural hair. It felt nice when she made perfect parts with her nails instead of reaching for the comb. The house smelled like heated avocado oil and the peppermint tea I made for us. I savored a few sips and tried to clear my head while Tasha gently worked through my hair.

Giana and I texted a little bit this afternoon, but our FiveStar group chat was dead. I hated having no idea where we stood. Were we fighting now? Was Riley still upset?

By the time Tasha started on my third cornrow, I was ready to fill her in on all the details.

"Everyone was going after one another, so I don't know why Riley got so upset," I wrapped up as Tasha tied off a fourth braid. "I'm just sad that it's affecting her so much."

"Well . . ." Tasha hummed through the hair clip poking out of her lip. "It seems like it's affecting all of you. And Riley is the odd one out. How would you feel if your friends linked up without you for a fun activity and you had to work with your parents, or work with me? I know I'm not some ol' head, but it still wouldn't be the same because I'm not one of your girls."

"You're my girl, Tasha! What are you talking about—" I was ready to come correct, but she cut me off.

"I know I'm your girl, Lay!" Tasha stopped so she could angle her face in my peripheral. "But I'm not part of FiveStar. I'm not part of that exclusive group. And that's okay, because it's for a reason."

Tasha was right. I loved her so much, and I thought of her like one of my girls. But she was family. We *were* friends, but not in the way that I was friends with Giana, Harper, Akila, and Riley.

"Look, Lay Lay," Tasha said, pulling me out of my head a little. "It sounds like you guys just need to talk it out and clear the air. You can work separately for the fair and still come together."

I knew she was right. It was just a matter of figuring out *how.*

The next day we all agreed to talk during lunch. So, nearly twenty-four hours after the mall moment, we circled up in the courtyard. As I looked around at my friends, it was hard not to notice that Riley didn't have a container of sweets today.

"I'm sorry, Riley," I said right away.

"I'm sorry, too—well, I mean, I'm not sorry about what I said," she explained. "But I'm sorry for snapping at you guys. It shouldn't have come out that way."

"I don't know, maybe it needed to," Harper admitted. "I'm sorry, too, Riley."

"Me too," Giana and Akila each chimed in.

"I mean, none of us really did anything wrong," Riley said. "I just feel like one second we were sharing booth ideas, and the next second we had three groups and I was alone. I didn't want to work by myself, but I didn't exactly tell you that, did I?"

Riley slowed to a stop. She played with the frayed end of her shoelace before meeting our eyes.

"Do you want to join one of our groups instead?" Akila asked carefully.

"No, not now," Riley said. "I'm doing what I want to do. It's not as fun without you guys, but I'm excited about my booth. My dad helped me hang up some flyers this morning. We already have eight people entering pies!"

"That's great, Riley!" Giana said, holding out a fist for her to bump.

"Is it true that Oscar Tomlinson is entering?" Harper asked, leaning in to whisper since Oscar was nearby with Terrell and Reggie.

"Yeah, I would not have taken him for a rhubarb guy," Riley said. We all cracked up.

"I'm a little afraid but also curious to see if it's actually good," I admitted.

"Oh, for *sure*," Akila said. "He's the type to secretly have *Great British Baking Show*–level skills."

I laughed. Suddenly it felt like things weren't as bad as I thought they had been. Tasha had been right—my friends just needed to come together and talk it out.

"Okay, so, for real," I said. "Clearly, the way things have been going isn't working. The way we were snapping at one another at the mall isn't like us."

"That's facts," Akila agreed.

"But we can't deny the fact that we all had points yesterday," Harper said. "There's overlap between our booths, and that's frustrating."

"Frustrating because . . . ?" Giana asked.

"Because the ideas are all good," Harper admitted. "And like Riley said, we all have to do what we think is best. But there *is* a part of me that feels weird about you using the tablecloth, the same way you feel weird about us using music and Riley feels weird about you guys having juice."

She was right. I didn't initially care about her and Akila using music at their booth, but it felt different after they went after Riley, and Riley snapped at me and Giana.

"So, it sounds like we have to eliminate the overlap," Riley said, looking at all of us.

"Yeah, but how?" I asked.

"We just . . . don't overlap?" Giana proposed. "Like, maybe we shouldn't talk about fair stuff anymore. We're all excited about one another's booths, but if the details are going to have us snapping, then maybe we just need to leave that out."

"So, we just *don't* talk about anything fair-related?" Riley asked.

"Yeah. We do fair work on fair time and do friend stuff on friend time," Giana explained. "We'll show up to the fair and be proud of one another, knowing no one stole an idea because we didn't exchange ideas to steal."

"That actually makes sense." Akila nodded. "I'm down."

"Me too," Harper said.

"Me three," Riley added, smiling.

They turned to me. Riley was okay. The weird energy had lifted. And like Akila said, Giana's idea made sense. But, even as I agreed to it, I wasn't sure if the idea was actually right.

·✦· CHAPTER 9 ·✦·

ON SATURDAY, GIANA HAD ALL four speakers out on my kitchen island, each organized with its own pile of equipment, waiting to be plugged into her computer for coding. I was on decoration duty, creating shiny glitter stars and cutting curtains from recycled fabric. Since Giana needed perfect silence for coding, I had my earbuds in, feeding me some Brandy and Monica. The smooth rhythm had me in a workflow so focused I didn't hear Giana calling my name until she was tapping me on the shoulder.

"My bad, girl," I said as I pulled out my earbuds.

"I wanted to show you the speakers," Giana said. "I coded them so the colors change with the beat. Slower songs will play cool tones like greens, blues, purples, and pink. Faster songs play hot colors like red, orange, and yellow. For songs with a mix of both, we'll just get an extra-cool show."

"That sounds dope! Let's see it in action."

I hit the lights, and Giana drew the curtains.

"What song should we play?" she asked, holding out the aux to me.

I plugged my phone in and opened the playlist I'd been listening to. Up next was "Best Friend," sung by Brandy. I pressed play.

I loved the way the sound filled the whole room, taking up all the empty space and cocooning us in Brandy's soprano harmonies.

"Best Friend" is on the long side. With the light show commanding my attention, my ears were left wide open to absorb the lyrics.

"What do you think everyone is doing today?" I asked Giana once the song had ended. I know I could just message the group chat and see for myself, but it felt weird. Even though I'd abide by our *no fair-talk* rule, it might be a bit much to work on the fair and try to have a fair-free conversation at the same time.

"I know Riley is helping her parents out at the farmer's market."

"That's probably a great place to recruit more people for her Bake-Off," I thought out loud.

"True . . . I bet she is."

I made my way to the fridge and pulled out a container of grapes and two sparkling waters. "I guess if Riley is at the farmer's market and we're here, Harper and Akila are probably working on their booth. Then again, Akila had gymnastics last night and they go late on Fridays sometimes—"

"She didn't have gymnastics last night," Giana corrected me.

"*Really?*" The last time Akila didn't go to gymnastics was when she hurt her ankle. She was the most dedicated athlete I knew.

"Yeah, she said the coach canceled so she had a free night."

I wondered if Giana was thinking the same thing as me. We could've had a sleepover on a Friday night for once!

"Why didn't she mention it?" I wondered aloud.

"When I asked Harper if she had any plans this weekend, she said she was getting together with Akila to work on their booth."

Even though that made sense, it felt all wrong at the same time.

"Five more days until the fair!" I loved the way my cousin Tasha had a way of waking up on the right side of the bed when she stayed over, but her enthusiasm was a little much for me on a Monday morning. I watched her start the coffee maker and pull a mug from the cabinet. I sat at the kitchen island sipping my green smoothie and eating breakfast, the hum of the coffee maker adding background noise to my music. Then my favorite Korey Vine song came on.

"Oh, can you turn that up? Pleaaaseeee," I asked before she sat down and I lost my chance. "I left my phone on the counter to charge."

Tasha reached for my phone and turned the volume up. My wireless speaker might not look as cool as Giana's, but it played Korey Vine's music just as well.

"I feel like I hear this song every five seconds." Tasha shook her head.

She brought her mug of coffee over to the island and sat down next to me.

"You know, I went to school with Korey Vine."

I slammed my hands down on the bench top, the only sensible thing to do short of stopping time and space.

"You *what*?"

"We weren't in the same grade, and we definitely weren't close, but I was in middle school when he was in high school—"

"Tasha—"

"Hey, it's closer than you or any of your friends have ever been!"

"I'm not coming for you right now!" I couldn't

help but clap on syllable. I needed her to listen. "I'm just trying to figure out why this is the first time I'm hearing about this. You gotta spill the tea."

"Hmmm. There isn't much to say. He was already pretty famous by the time I was old enough to understand all the hype. I just remember everyone would talk about him and he would travel a lot."

"Did you ever meet him or see him?"

"When we had the Almost High School program, I was in his tour group," she said like it's no big deal that *Korey Vine* gave her a tour of Woodlawn High School.

"That's amazing," I assured her, wondering what else she might think wasn't a big deal or worth sharing.

"He had no idea who I was, Lay," she said, smiling. "It was cool, though. It was also cool that he did that kind of thing, you know? Like, he was already a full-blown celebrity, but he still wanted to give school tours to underclassmen. I respect that. I don't respect the fact that I've heard the same song a kajillion times in less than a week, but I respect his ethics."

"Stop shuffling your playlists then," I said, giving her a shove.

"I still want to hear new music, just not if every other song is one of his," she whined.

"Okay, that's fair, that's fair."

"You know, you're like him that way. I feel like most kids your age could get caught up. You're *That Girl Lay Lay*, but you choose to be yourself, to just be Lay Lay. And Lay Lay shows up for her friends and her community. You stay grounded. There are some adults who don't know how to do that."

"*You* just told *me* that *I'm* like *Korey Vine*," I gushed, not ready to move past that yet.

"Oh gosh, don't let it go to your head."

"Too late!" I said as I twirled out of the kitchen on cloud nine.

·✦· CHAPTER 10 ·✦·

WITH FOUR MORE DAYS UNTIL the fair, Ms. Ortega and a few other teachers let us use class time to build our booths. When Harper and I arrived for class, Riley was already there, going to town with a base coat on a large wooden sign.

"Hey, Riley," I said.

"Whatcha working on?" Harper asked.

"Hey, guys. I'm—uh—painting a sign for my booth."

"I can't wait to see how it turns out," I admitted.

"Honestly, I can," Riley said, grimacing. "I am *not* an artist, not by a long shot."

"Well—" I stopped myself from suggesting she ask Akila or Harper for help. I know how to do layout and design, but painting is more their thing. I glanced at Harper, but she was looking at something across the room.

"I'm sure it'll be great." I tried to sound encouraging.

When Giana and Akila showed up, we split off into our groups.

Giana and I needed to build a frame to hang our curtain and decorations. One of the parent volunteers helped us connect all the wood with power tools. From there, it was up to us to paint!

"Are you using the pink and blue, Riley?" I asked.

"No, it's all yours," Riley said.

"It's coming together," I said encouragingly as I glanced at her sign.

"I guess," she said slowly. "I just want it to be good . . ."

She glanced in Akila and Harper's direction. They were sitting on the floor with a notebook between them. Akila tapped the page with her pen before covering her face with her hands.

"I wonder what that's about," I said.

"They've been trying to figure out a playlist," Riley said matter-of-factly.

"I thought they were going to play Nigerian music."

"I think they still are, but Harper suggested they throw in a few mainstream songs, but neither of them know how to create a flow . . . at least that's what I picked up on."

"Oh . . ." I *loved* making playlists. I could go over and offer to help—

"Did you come over here for something?" Riley asked, wiping some paint off her chin.

"Right, yes—pink and blue paint, please!"

Riley handed me the paints and a few brushes. I brought them over to Giana, who was busy typing away on her laptop.

"More coding?"

She looked up at me, pushed her glasses up on her nose, and smiled.

"No. I thought we should figure out our

signature refreshment," Giana admitted, turning her computer around. She had an Excel spreadsheet filled with different recipe combinations. "Not many people make smoothie *juice* like our dude at the mall. So to get that chunk-less thickness, we might have to experiment."

"We could ask Riley. With all those compotes and reductions, she probably knows what we should do."

"Yeaaaahhh . . ." Giana turned her computer back around. "I don't want to rock the boat, you know? Like, she was so sensitive about it at the mall, and now we're all, like, in a good place."

As much as I wanted to argue, Giana was right. Things had cooled down, and with the fair this weekend, we were *this close* to getting back to normal . . .

But I didn't feel good. Between our smoothie juice dilemma, Riley's lack of painting skills, and Harper and Akila's playlist problem, it seemed like the fair still had enough power to pull us apart.

Wednesday afternoon when school let out for early release, Giana, Harper, Akila, Riley, and I rode the bus with a few teachers and some other students to the food bank's temporary home at Woodlawn Baptist.

We headed into the gym, which was where the food bank had set up its temporary operation. Metal shelves lined each wall, and the center of the room had two lines of tables with people organizing boxes and bags of food.

Ms. Ortega introduced us to the lead volunteer for our shift, a woman named Ivanna. She wore bright orange leggings, a gray Woodlawn Food Bank Volunteer T-shirt, and a smile bright enough to be a statement piece. I instantly knew we would vibe.

"Okay, welcome to the temporary Woodlawn Food Bank," Ivanna said. "Today, I'll split you into groups. The goal is to unload boxes onto the shelves. If you have questions and can't find me, anyone wearing a gray shirt should be able to help you."

Ivanna called out names and sent us to different stations—condiments, dry goods, pasta, soup mixes—the list went on and on.

"Now, Akila, Alaya, Giana, Harper, and Riley, I'll take you to canned goods and get you started," Ivanna said.

We followed her to the far corner of the gym where three tables with stacks of boxes were waiting.

"Everything is already organized, so when you finish unloading one box, just move on to the next. I'll leave you to it!"

We each grabbed a box and claimed a shelf.

In the quiet, it was tempting to turn the soft sound of cans landing on the shelves or clinking together into a beat. But I wasn't in the mood to rap. My thoughts drifted to the food bank. On the bus ride over, Ms. Ortega was talking about how it was an important community resource, and without it some people wouldn't have reliable access to food.

I was lucky. I'd never had to go without food, and I couldn't imagine what that might be like, especially for a kid. Whenever my stomach started growling, there was something around to eat. But what if there was nothing?

"Honestly, I'm thinking about the kids who have to eat this stuff," I admitted to my friends as I looked down at the can of string beans in my hand. It didn't look very appetizing, but it was still food. And sometimes that was all that really counted.

"You know, I was kinda thinking about that when she called out the groups," Harper admitted. "There isn't a snack section. And I get that snacks aren't *everything*, but—I don't know . . ."

"I wonder if we can donate snacks," I said, the idea popping into my head. "The kind of snacks *kids* like."

"I'm pretty sure we can," Akila said.

"Oh! We could go all out with it," Riley suggested, getting amped. "I could have my parents take us to Save A Lot so we could get a lot of everything."

"And we could stop at Planet of Pizza since it's next door," Giana added. "I haven't been there in *forever*."

"Oh yeah!" I chimed in. "That pizza is magic."

"Okay, okay. So, Planet of Pizza and bulk candy for the kids," Harper said, laughing. "It's a date."

"I feel like people don't always think about that kind of stuff," Giana mused. "Like when you donate to a food bank you're thinking things that'll last, staples, cans, dry goods, and so on. But who thinks about the kids?"

"Sometimes it takes a kid to think like a kid," Riley said.

We picked up our empty boxes and headed back to the table for new ones. I realized this was the first time we had laughed together in a week. Then I had another realization. My friends and I were working together today like a team, and we're *always* better that way.

"I don't think *not* talking about the fair was the right decision," I admitted out loud. "Riley, Giana and I could really use your help getting the consistency right for our smoothie juice. Our drink could even be a teaser to get people interested in your booth. And you could ask Akila or Harper to help paint your booth since they're so artistic."

I turned to Akila and Harper and took a deep breath.

"And I *know* you two need help with the playlist for your booth. I'm great at making playlists! And I want to help you guys because it'll bring more people to your booth and raise more money for the food bank. That's what we're trying to do at the end of the day."

My friends were quiet as I waited for their reactions. In a way, I realized my friends and I were like the branches of a tree. Alone, we grew in different directions, into our own unique strengths. But the branches came together at the trunk. That was our friendship, and it was strong enough to support all of us if we let it!

"I forgot about that," Riley said quietly. "Part of me was hurt when we split up. I'm excited about the pie Bake-Off, but when you guys all wanted to work with one another, I thought my idea wasn't good enough. I felt like I had something to prove."

"Riley!" We all came in for a group hug.

"Your idea is awesome," Akila assured her.

"I actually have another idea for your booth, Riley," Giana said. "I started coding a program so people can scan a QR code and vote for pies on their phones. Then you can have a live feed of the votes. We can give all the contestants code names so the winner is still a surprise."

"That would be great, Giana," Riley said,

beaming. "I was dreading having to count the votes by myself."

"Lay Lay, we actually thought it might be cool to play your music at our booth," Harper chimed in. "When people ask who's singing, we can send them to your karaoke booth."

Riley smiled. "If we ask for booths next to one another, we can create a little flow. Anyone who gets full from pie at my booth can go try some batik or karaoke. And if people get parched from singing and try the smoothie juice samples, you can tell them there's more to eat and drink at my booth!"

I could see it. We would be working together while doing our own things—it was the perfect solution!

"This is going to be great!" I said. And for the first time in a minute, I really meant it.

·✦· CHAPTER 11 ·✦·

AS WE HEADED BACK TO the bus after volunteering, Riley and I continued to talk about smoothie juice.

We both stopped and turned around when we heard someone call my name.

"Lay Lay? *That Girl Lay Lay?*"

I followed the voice and locked eyes with a girl who had perfectly laid edges.

"Oh my gosh, it's really *her!*" She rushed over to me along with two friends. The girls were all a little younger than us, and they wore matching lightning bolt earrings. They reminded me of me and my friends.

"Hey!" I said. "What's up?" I was always ready to bring my best energy when I ran into fans.

"We love your music," said a girl with blue-and-purple braces.

"We were hoping you'd take a picture with us," the third girl said. Her curly hair and freckles reminded me of Riley.

"Sure thing!" I turned to Riley and raised my brows, silently asking if she'd take the pic. The first girl handed her phone to me, and I passed it off to Riley. "Thank you!"

As we figured out a pose, I asked, "What are your names?"

"I'm Tobi," the first girl said.

"I'm Aspen," said the girl with braces.

"And I'm Monica." The third girl blushed a bit.

"Cool, it's nice to meet you guys!"

The four of us gathered for a sassy pose. I knew we looked cute!

"Thank you, Lay Lay," Monica said. I held out my fist for her to bump.

"Yeah, this was so cool," Tobi gushed.

As the girls huddled around the phone, I looked over at Riley and figured this was our opening to leave.

"Wait!" Aspen called out.

"What's up, girl?" I asked.

"Would you . . . Would it be too much to ask you to freestyle?" she asked. "Like you did in that video?"

"That depends," I said. "Can you give me a beat?"

She looked at her friends before nodding at me. I turned to Riley to make sure she was cool waiting a little longer. The bus wasn't leaving yet, so we had a few minutes.

"You got this, Lay!" she said, smiling.

Tobi started a little one-two step, stomping her feet. I was feeling it, finding the rhythm. Aspen came in, clapping her hands. Monica started rubbing her knuckles together, making an unexpected washboard-like sound. I realized she was rubbing artificial nails together, taking the beat over the top!

I got in the zone and counted the beat. *One—two—*

HEY, Y'ALL, I'M THAT GIRL LAY LAY
I'M OUT HERE FOR MY SCHOOL'S VOLUNTEER DAY
LISTEN CLOSE CUZ I'M HERE TO LET YOU KNOW
THE WOODLAWN FOOD BANK HELPS
THE COMMUNITY GROW
IT'S WHAT WE'RE HERE TO SAVE BY
WORKING TOGETHER
ADJUSTING TO CHANGE CAN HELP US DO BETTER
NOW IS THE TIME TO STAND UP AND SAY
WOODLAWN FOOD BANK IS HERE TO STAY
SO, COME TO THE SCHOOL FAIR IF YOU DARE
PLAY SOME GAMES AND TAKE SOME NAMES
AND HELP WOODLAWN FOOD BANK SEE ANOTHER DAY
GOT MY GIRLS WITH ME AND WE CAME TO SLAY
SO, JOIN US AND SAVE THE FOOD BANK, 'AYE!

As I found the words, more kids and a few adults came outside to listen. I got louder and danced a little bit, pumping my arms to hype up the crowd. By the end, everyone was clapping. I told them if they wanted to see a longer performance and help the food bank, they should come to opening night at the Woodlawn Middle School Fair.

96

"I can't wait to see you all there!" I shouted.

As the small crowd spread out, my friends caught up to me.

"That was great, Lay Lay," Riley said, clapping me on the shoulder.

"Yeah, way to get the word out *and* give a boss performance," Harper said.

"You stay ready, girl," Akila said as she looped her arm around my shoulder for a squeeze. "I love that about you."

Harper's words played again in my head, reminding me of what Tasha said about Korey Vine being more than a celebrity. I realized maybe I *could* be doing something more to help save the food bank.

When I got home, I brought Tasha up to speed on my plan: a three-day campaign to spread the word about the fair through my social media. The more people we got to show up, the more money we would raise!

"Riley filmed my freestyle at the church, so that'll be today's post. Then I'll use some of the pictures I took of everyone's booths in progress for tomorrow. And I can design a virtual flyer by Friday. I wish I'd thought of it sooner, but I think this is the best way to make the most of the time we have left!"

I took a beat, watching Tasha's expression as she chewed on her pesto rotini across from me.

"Thoughts?" I asked eagerly.

"Well, there might be an even better way," she said, pushing her shoulders back and beaming at me with a smile brighter than the full moon. "I was able to get you face time with *Korey Vine!*"

I opened my mouth but nothing came out. I wanted to pinch myself to make sure this wasn't a crazy dream.

"If you want, you guys are doing an Instagram Live tomorrow night," Tasha explained. "It's just a casual conversation comparing experiences as kid stars, but this could be great visibility for you and the fair."

"Thank you, thank you, THANK YOU!" I gushed

when I could talk again. I got up from my stool and ran around the island to give her a hug. "How'd you pull this off? I'm in shock."

"Well, our conversation the other day reminded me how down-to-earth Korey is. So, I reached out to his mom on Facebook. She and my mom were pretty close back when I was a kid. We caught up, and I *might* have mentioned how you reminded me of Korey. I said I thought it would be great for you to talk to someone who's been where you are."

"That's incredible, Tasha," I told her. "Seriously, how do I thank you?"

"Well, you could remind me that I'm the most amazing cousin in the world," Tasha crossed her arms and smiled. "I expect to see that printed on a mug sometime in the near future."

"Humility looks great on you, Tash," I said, laughing a little.

"Really brings out my eyes, doesn't it?"

On Thursday evening, instead of washing up for bed, I got glammed up for an Instagram Live with *Korey Vine!*

With my space buns on point and a little lip gloss, the last piece to my look was the FiveStar hoodie Akila designed for me and my friends when we performed in the school talent show. The hoodie is a symbol of our friendship and how bright we shine together—five stars instead of one. I ran my fingers over the clear rhinestones outlining a star and the number five. Maybe Akila could design some batik stuff for us once the fair was over!

I wiped off my phone while Tasha grabbed my ring light, and with thirty seconds to spare she backed out of my room flashing me a thumbs-up.

"You got this, Lay!" she said. "And remember to have fun."

"Thanks, Tasha."

She closed my door, and I knew she'd watch on her phone in the other room. My friends said they'd log in, too.

One moment, I was sitting in my room, triple-checking my makeup and adjusting my earrings.

The next, I tapped my Instagram Live invite and split my phone screen with the Korey Vine!

"Whaddup, whaddup! It's ya boy, Korey, and I'm so excited to finally get the chance to chat with my girl, my hometown homie, That Girl Lay Lay!"

"Hey, Korey! Hey, y'all," I said, smiling so hard my cheeks were already getting sore.

We got straight to it. Korey asked me about growing up in Woodlawn pre–viral video, and I was ready. He said since coming home he noticed not a lot had changed, which was a good thing. I couldn't believe it! Korey Vine was in Woodlawn.

Since Korey was from Woodlawn and started his career around my age, we compared notes on what it was like getting into the music industry so young. Since he got his start before social media was a thing, acting got his foot in the door. I had no idea!

After a while, we answered questions from fans in the comments. I cheesed extra hard when I saw Harper's and Riley's names pop up.

"For real, this was a dope convo," Korey said, starting to close out the event. "I'm glad we finally got to connect, and we *definitely* gotta link up onstage sometime."

I knew that was my cue to say something positive, agreeing that we gotta link up "someday." But my eyes darted to the top of the screen and I could see thousands of people watching, thousands of people who got the notification that he was going live and wanted to come show support. Thousands of people who might show up at the fair . . .

"Actually," I said, weighing the risk. This would either be one of my best ideas or a complete flop, but it was worth a try. If what Tasha said about Korey being down-to-earth and caring about his community was true, then he might *want* to help us. "I'm performing at the Woodlawn Middle School Fair this Saturday. If you want, since you're in town, we could share the stage then."

"Yo!" Korey said. "The middle school fair, that's whaddup."

"All the money we raise is going to help keep the Woodlawn Food Bank open. The more people who come, the more help we can give."

"Wow . . ." He trailed off, shaking his head and

looking off-screen. I couldn't tell if it was a good *wow* or a bad *wow*, but either way I put it out there and that was all I could do.

Korey collected himself and looked at the camera again. "You know, when I was younger, sometimes my mom would have to get us food there. I didn't really understand it back then, but for her that was a saving grace. We prolly wouldn't have had food sometimes without it. Lay Lay, I'll be there!"

"Awesome! Thank you, Korey." I had to keep myself from full-on gushing, but the likes flooding the screen and comments coming in asking where the fair was and how much people could donate made it hard not to fall out of my chair.

"I gotchu, sis! And y'all heard it here first. I'm gonna be performing at the Woodlawn Middle School Fair this Saturday with That Girl Lay Lay. I know it's a lil last minute, but if you can, pull up, have some fun, and show support. Ya heard?"

I signed off, and Tasha was at my door a second later.

"Look at you!" she gushed, wrapping me in a hug. "Performing with Korey Vine. Making career moves *and* helping the food bank! Lay Lay, I want to be like *you* when I grow up."

I laughed. I was still buzzing from the news. There were still a lot of details to figure out. Even so, no matter what, this was big—for me *and* for Woodlawn! It was moments like this that made me wonder, *What was my life?!*

·✦· CHAPTER 12 ·✦·

I WOKE UP ON FRIDAY to a ton of notifications.
Korey posted the live feed from last night and tagged
me. People were liking and commenting, asking for
details, and following my account, too. Korey had
also emailed me a list of his songs with female fea-
tures I could step in on, so I had some practicing to
do! It was going to be an intense few days.

"Congrats, Lay Lay," Sofia said when I arrived at
school.

"Thanks, girl!"

"Hey, Lay Lay, good look getting Korey Vine to come to the fair!" Oscar held out a fist for me to bump as he rolled by on his Heelys. "That's gonna be dope."

"Oscar! Wheels up!" Mr. LaCourt, our math teacher, shouted not two seconds later. I couldn't help but laugh a little.

I rounded the corner and found my friends waiting at my locker. They were huddled together looking at something.

"What's poppin'?" I asked.

They all snapped around, and Giana grabbed my hands and started doing this excited running-in-place thing. Harper hugged my shoulders, and Akila hugged my waist.

"Lay Lay!" Riley said, smiling hard. She held her phone out for me to see. They were looking at social media posts about Korey and my performance. "This is so big! I mean, it is big, right? Like for you, for your career?"

"It is," I said, adjusting my jean jacket after my friends finally let me go. "And it's big for the fair and the food bank, too."

"How did you know he was gonna say yes?" Akila asked.

"I didn't . . . I just *really* hoped he would."

"It would have been his loss if he said no," Giana said. "Just think about it: Korey's fans are coming on top of the people who already knew about the fair—"

"On *top* of *your* fans, too, Lay Lay," Akila reminded me.

"Right!" I smiled. "With that many people, we have a real shot at saving the food bank!"

With Korey on the books and opening night the next day, we had no choice but to call an emergency sleepover so we could get all our booths ready to go.

Giana made a checklist, and Riley made snacks. Then my friends and I made a bed of pillows and blankets for when we were ready to wind down at the end of the night.

Riley and Giana finished designing the poll program for the pie competition. I helped Akila and Harper mix a playlist for the batik experience with some of my own songs mixed in. We all made extra decorations for all three booths. Then we headed to the kitchen in time for Riley to pull her final test pie out of the oven. While the pie cooled, we pulled fruit from the fridge and got to work making smoothie juice and taste testing the options.

"Well, it's no Bahama Berry, but I think this is the winner," I mused, pausing to lick the blood orange-mango-strawberry blend off my lips. "I'm going to call it Citrus Sing."

"Oh, great name, Lay!" Giana said. "And it fits the theme of our booth."

"I love it," Akila said decidedly, setting down her glass with a soft tink.

As Giana and I stacked jars of Citrus Sing in the fridge for the next day, Riley finally cut into her pie. The loud whirring of the blender was replaced with the sound of forks scraping plates as we devoured Riley's peach masterpiece.

"I want my house to smell like brown sugar,

cinnamon, and peaches forever." I sighed, gesturing to the air with my fork.

"You've outdone yourself, Riley," Harper said. She held up her free hand to rain down some poetry snaps.

"I have a good feeling this is going to be the best Woodlawn Middle School Fair *ever*," Giana guessed.

"I expect nothing less," Akila agreed, tapping her fork against Giana's.

Saturday was fair day! As tempting as it had been to stay up and watch a movie the night before, we had all fallen asleep quickly. Everyone got picked up super early the next morning and I started getting glammed up for my performance. A trip to Selma's Salon and a home visit from my hairdresser had me looking the part a few hours later.

As I spun around in front of my mirror, double- and triple-checking my outfit, I realized I had really found a way to use my music to help Woodlawn. I used to think that rapping was something I did because I was good at it. But freestyling about the food bank helped raise awareness. If everything worked out, then Korey *and* my music would really make a difference.

Tasha gave me and Giana a ride over to the fair an hour before opening.

Ms. Ortega found us in the parking lot before Tasha had a chance to put the car in park.

"Hello, girls!" She marked something off on her clipboard and handed me a sheet of paper. "Okay, this is a map of the fairgrounds. Your booth is over here. The stage is assembled as requested, so all you have to do is add your decorations. Oh, and, Lay Lay: You can stop by the stage in about an hour for sound check. The performances start at six."

Giana, Tasha, and I grabbed the rest of the speakers and mics from the trunk and followed the map to our spot, passing a mini Ferris wheel and a spinning teacup ride on the way. We passed Sofia and a couple of her friends setting up a huge wheel with categories like *Wicked*, *Hamilton*, and *The Lion King* for their trivia booth. And Oscar waved at us from where he and his mom were setting up his dunk tank.

"Are we almost there?" Giana asked, her voice muffled behind the two speakers she was carrying.

"I think so," I said. The field was bigger than it looked.

"Hey, watch out!"

I stopped and looked up from the map just in time to see a crate of basketballs in front of me.

"That would've been bad," Reggie said, running over to move the crate.

"Thanks for the save," I said, truly grateful. Tripping right now would have been a disaster!

"It's the least we can do," Terrell said as he stepped down from the ladder he was using to hang three basketball hoops in front of a mural of an outdoor basketball court.

"Beatbox and Basketball," Giana read aloud from a sign painted in graffiti lettering.

"Yup, combining two of the best things into one irresistible activity," Terrell said, crossing his arms and bucking his chin.

"Well, you're not wrong," I admitted.

After a quick good-bye, we kept moving.

"Hey, what did that kid mean by 'it's the least we can do'?" Tasha asked.

"Oh, he was probably talking about a competition we have going on," Giana said, rolling her eyes.

"What competition?"

Giana and I told Tasha about the boys stealing our oak tree and the challenge to outearn one another at the fair. I guess one good thing about it is that the competition had pushed all of us to do the most to help the food bank.

When we got to our booth, I hung the curtains and string lights while Giana set up the speakers along the edge of the stage. Tasha helped us run lines from the screen and mics so we could get power from the generator. We finished in record time and stood back to admire our work.

"I don't know. Win or lose, you guys did a great job," Tasha said. "Just know that, okay?"

"We know," I said, smiling at Giana.

Akila and Harper showed up next, and we helped them set up all their dye and batik gear. Akila wore a short-sleeve shirt dyed the deepest shade of purple I'd ever seen. The way her braids fell, it was the perfect shade to make her gold beads pop. She and Harper hung a batik tapestry across the back of their booth.

"Did you guys make this?" Giana asked as we looked at the stars dyed into the fabric.

"We did," Harper admitted. "It was so cool. Akila definitely has to show you guys how to do batik sometime."

"I'm down!" I agreed easily. "Maybe we can come over to your booth for a quick lesson later!"

People started arriving with glassware and baking dishes of pie for Riley's Bake-Off. Tasha and I directed people on where to put their pies.

"I wonder where Riley is—" I began, when Riley and her parents suddenly appeared, winded from the rush.

"Thanks for helping!" Riley gasped as she unloaded her own pies. "I know I'm late, but I had to make sure these pies were perfect."

"No worries, Riles," Giana told her. "We got your back."

When we finished setting up, we had three great booths side by side.

"Wow! Look at this," Ms. Ortega shouted. "Great job, girls. I am so impressed! And I'm definitely going to stop by to sample some of those pies. It smells *heavenly* over here."

"When you do, I can show you how to vote for your favorite from your phone, Ms. Ortega," Riley said, glancing over to smile at Giana.

"Excellent! Well, I'm making the rounds and letting everyone know that we open the gates in five minutes. I'll be back around throughout the night. Don't forget to have fun!"

Akila's dad took out his phone.

"Let's get a picture of you all together," he said.

The other parents—plus my amazing cousin Tasha—pulled out their phones, too.

My girls and I gathered together in Riley's booth to pose. I had my arms around Giana and Akila's shoulders, so I gave them a squeeze. They did the same, and soon we were all giggling.

"Smile and say 'pie'!" Akila's dad said.

"Dad!" Akila groaned. The rest of us just giggled and went along with it.

"PIE!" we shouted all together.

I just knew this was going to be an amazing night.

✦ CHAPTER 13 ✦

JUST MINUTES LATER, THE FAIR was in full swing. People walked around, checking out the booths and playing games. While we waited for our first customers, Giana played music videos on our giant screen. We didn't get through the first song before people started lining up to sing!

When the first performance began and the speakers started changing colors, I realized how well it had all come together. By the time our first two customers were done, we had a long line.

"I need to find something to drink," I overheard one of them say.

"I know, my throat is kinda dry after that."

Giana stepped up with our tray of Citrus Sing samples.

"This is amazing," one of the women said, drawing the attention of some of the other people in line. "You only have samples?"

"Yup. We have samples, but if you want more, you can get a full cup at the pie Bake-Off booth," I explained, pointing down to where Riley was working her own crowd.

"Oh! Great, thank you!"

They headed toward Riley and the next group stepped up for their turn. The flow had begun!

We'd hit the ground running. We might not have been working at the same booth, but we *were* working together, all parts of a greater whole. And it was paying off! I barely had a chance to look up or check on Harper, Akila, and Riley as Giana and I collected tons of tickets.

I don't know how much time passed, but I turned to the next person in line and found our friends holding out two full cups of Citrus Sing.

"Hey, guys! Just wanted to come over and say we are killing it," Riley said, holding up her cup.

Giana and I held ours up, too, and we all toasted.

"To an awesome turnout," Akila started.

"To catching a breath," Harper added.

"To us pulling this off," Giana said.

"And to us, period," I finished, all of us taking a sip.

I noticed the line in front of our booth dividing. I thought we were about to lose customers, but then a familiar face popped up behind my girls.

"Hey, I heard the famous That Girl Lay Lay was running the baddest booth at this thing," Korey Vine said, smiling. He was fresh with a clean fade and box braids hanging down to his cheeks.

Korey stepped to the front, flanked by his posse.

"Hey, Korey!" I said, bumping the fist he held out to me.

"Yo, the fair is fire. I forgot how clever y'all kids could be. There's a Broadway trivia *wheel*," he said, leaning down so I could hear him over the crowd.

"Sofia would be so excited if you stopped by

her booth," I told him, trying to keep my cool.

"Noted," he said, nodding his head and taking a second to look around. "Y'all got a whole operation here?" he asked, gesturing to our three booths.

"I guess we do! Giana and I are running the karaoke booth. Akila and Harper are teaching people how to batik, and Riley's selling Citrus Sing and tastes of pie."

"Citrus Sing? Wait, is that the orange strawberry stuff people been talking about?"

"That's the one!" Riley chimed in.

"That's where we're heading next," Korey said to his friends.

A crowd had formed around us. A few people close by heard he was about to leave and started to protest.

"You guys should sing something!"

"Please, there are mics right there—"

"Yeah, won't you sing for us?"

Korey lifted his arms above his head to get everyone's attention. The crowd was quick to get quiet, probably hoping he was about to perform right then.

"We're performing at the top of the hour, ya'll," he explained. "We savin' our voices. But don't worry. I promise you'll get to see us soon. In the meantime, check out these dope booths! Enjoy yourselves, and I'll see you at the stage."

The crowd clapped and Korey turned around to give us a wink before he followed Riley back to her booth. Korey's visit made us even more popular, so we all rushed back to our spots and kicked it up a notch.

In no time at all, Tasha came by to tell me it was time for my sound check.

"Good luck, Lay Lay!" Giana said.

I quickly made my way to the stage. There was a plain white backdrop flanked with lights and speakers. We walked around the platform, passing a few tech people setting up lights and Korey's bodyguards. They were dressed in black and standing shoulder to shoulder like a brick wall, but they let us through.

"Oh my goodness." Ms. Ortega rushed over to us with the band teacher, Dr. Lieberman, close behind. They both looked frazzled.

"Ms. Ortega, what's going on?"

"Something's wrong with the speakers," she explained breathlessly. "I don't know what's going on, but without sound we can't do a sound *check*."

"They're not making *any* sound?" Tasha asked.

"No," Dr. Lieberman replied. "I took a look and Korey has his people on it right now, but we still haven't figured it out."

"What are we going to do? Without speakers Korey and Lay Lay won't be able to perform!"

Ms. Ortega covered her face with her hands.

"It's okay, we still have some time," Tasha said. "We'll figure something out."

What, though? Like Ms. Ortega said, people had showed up because of Korey, and now they wouldn't be able to hear him sing. What if people started leaving? That wouldn't be good for the fair, and that definitely wouldn't be good for the food bank. I *had* to do something—

"I'll be right back, okay?" I said. "There's someone who might be able to help us."

I pushed through the crowd and ran back to the karaoke booth. With the show set to start soon, everyone was catching a break, including my girls.

"Giana, I need your help," I huffed, out of breath. I gripped the table, grabbing her water bottle and taking a few sips.

"Whoa, what's going on?" she asked, standing up immediately.

"Something's wrong with the speakers on the stage. They aren't working. And without speakers, we can't perform, and without the performance people might leave, and—"

"Come on, I can look at them," Giana said, reaching below our table for the tool kit she packed in case we needed any last-minute fixes on our own speakers.

Our parents agreed to watch our booths while my friends and I headed back to the stage. We quickly came up with a plan. Giana told the security guards I sent her so she could get to the stage and work on the speakers. In the meantime, Akila, Harper, Riley, and I would buy her some time.

We pushed toward the front of the crowd,

holding hands so we didn't lose one another. We stopped once we reached the stage and huddled close together.

"Are you sure about this, Lay Lay?" Riley asked.

"Yeah, everyone is here to see celebrities, not—"

"We've got this," Harper jumped in before I could. She looked at all of us, her eyes sharp and bright. "We told Giana we'd buy her time. We've gotta have her back."

"For sure," Riley said.

I felt a surge of pride. My friends and I, we were showing up for one another, and for all the work our classmates had done for the fair and the food bank.

We pulled apart and turned to face the crowd, catching a few people's attention. I counted us off, loud enough that we turned more heads, and on "one" we started singing "Best Friend" by Brandy. We harmonized and used a routine we played around with at our last sleepover.

"It's That Girl Lay Lay!" someone shouted. "She and her friends are singing!"

By the time we were halfway through the song,

the crowd had spread out a little to give us some room and they were clapping on beat.

We moved around one another, doing our own version of an electric slide during the chorus. Then we shifted so each of us ended up in front for a verse.

Harper went first, swaying her shoulders and stepping into a quick running man. She did a slow shimmy, letting the motion move her to the back of the group. Akila was next. She brought some extra energy when the beat picked up, doing a couple jump turns and popping her shoulders on beat.

The grass made it easy to do some sliding foot-work, so Riley busted out with one of the smoothest moonwalks I've seen! I cupped my hands.

"Go, Riley! Go, Riley!" I chanted loudly.

The crowd got into it and started cheering, too. Riley snapped her fingers and moonwalked back into line with us. I was saving up my energy for the stage, but I pumped my arms and worked the crowd. People were singing along, the sound so loud I almost couldn't hear us anymore!

Akila finished us off with a backflip, landing in a split that made the crowd cheer.

Almost on the dot, everyone's faces lit up. A few people held up their hands to shield their eyes, but I knew what that meant. The stage lights were on, which was Giana's signal that we were good to go!

"Hey, everyone!" I shouted to grab their attention. "I'm That Girl Lay Lay, and these are my friends Harper, Akila, and Riley. The main event starts in just a few minutes!"

With that, we grabbed hands and filed around the edge of the stage.

"You did it!" I said when we caught up with Giana.

"Yes! The speakers were fine, but the wire connecting them to power was bad," she explained, blushing a little.

"Girl, you saved the show," I gushed. "Thank you, thank you, thank you!"

We all squeezed Giana in a group hug. I was buzzing with energy from our performance and for what was to come.

Tasha found us and handed back Giana's tools. "Lay Lay, we gotta get you through sound check. You're the first one to go on."

"You got this, Lay," Akila said.

"We'll be in the front row!" Riley chimed in.

"Break a leg, girl." Giana smiled at me.

"Bring that fire!" Harper cheered.

I headed off with Tasha. Once I was fitted for my mic and we were all set, I took a deep breath and hit the stage for my performance.

·◆·· CHAPTER 14 ··◆·

THE SHOW WAS ON POINT. I did my solo set first and got a break when Korey went on to perform a few songs from his new album. He took the stage and the lights got brighter while his voice boomed through the speakers like thunder. The sound of the crowd cheering rivaled the stage speakers' top volume.

"You did this, hon," Tasha told me while I was backstage. "You put this together. I've never seen a turnout like this."

Korey's stage director let me know it was time to

go back out. The crowd had doubled since my performance, which meant the number of people at the fair was off the charts!

"For the first time, it's ya boy Korey Vine taking the stage with That Girl Lay Lay!" Korey announced, drawing out my name as I joined him.

Since we didn't have time for an official rehearsal, the stage director had instructed us to keep the moves simple and focus on working the crowd instead. I was cool with it!

Korey started the song, coming in soft and cueing me for my harmonies. I made my way to the front of the stage and got everyone swaying with the soulful rhythm. We sang together on the chorus and when it was time, I shifted over to center stage for my rap verse. I had a full solo in one of Korey's songs! I'd rehearsed a hundred times in the last two days, and I delivered my lines perfectly now. Korey caught my eye and flashed a thumbs-up. I saw my friends up front and waved to them, cheesin' hard and not caring at all. It was incredible!

When the applause died down and I'd caught my breath, I stepped forward.

"Thank you for coming to the Woodlawn Middle School Fair! I'm excited to share the stage with Korey tonight and have the opportunity to lift up Woodlawn together.

"If you didn't know, this year's fair is supporting the Woodlawn Food Bank. Recently, a tree fell, badly damaging the building's roof. The money raised here at the fair will go to repair the building so they can get back up and running. Without the Woodlawn Food Bank, many people wouldn't have access to what they need. So, get your tickets, have fun, and support the community!"

After the performance, I caught up with my girls at Akila and Harper's booth when I heard a familiar voice behind me.

"Congrats on your performance," Reggie said. "It was cool to see you up there, and you got to perform with *Korey Vine*."

I could tell from his tone he was geeking out a little.

"Yeah, it was cool . . . you know," Terrell added.

"Thanks, guys," I said, making a mental note to stop by their booth before the night was over so I could shoot some hoops.

"Y'all should be congratulating us on winning, too," Akila added.

"Uh, the tickets haven't been counted yet," Terrell pointed out. "So, we don't know who won—"

"Actually, *we* won," Harper said, smiling.

"Since we split up to work on our booths, we collectively have almost a thousand tickets," Riley explained.

"And I did the math," Giana added. "Based on how many tickets per person, and how many people can play your game at one time, *and* how long each turn is, it's physically impossible for you to catch up to us."

My jaw hit the floor. I couldn't believe what I was hearing, but in the best way.

"When did y'all figure this out?" I asked my girls.

"While you were performing," Akila replied.

"Yo—"

"What?!"

The boys groaned, but Terrell stepped forward. "All right, all right, you get to have your tree."

"Y'all deserve it," Reggie admitted.

"Thanks," Riley said. "And you guys should tell Brendon his apple pie is clearly going to win. He's a pretty amazing baker."

I turned to congratulate my friends on our unofficial victory, excited to have our tree back. But I was interrupted *again*—this time by Korey Vine himself.

"Whoa, whoa, whoa! What are y'all doin' over here?" he said. "I came to tear it up in some kara-oh-kay." The way he sounded it out had us laughing.

"Unless you're scared," he added.

My eyebrows hit the roof. I turned to my girls, and they nodded at me in support. We already knew we had this in the bag.

"You really want to go up against FiveStar, Korey?" I asked, crossing my arms.

"Oh, I'm ready!"

We headed over to our booth. Korey's people jumped in, ready with some extra mics since there were so many of us.

Since the sun had gone down, our speakers shone bright and the colors turned our stage into a light show. We were a few songs in when Ms. Ortega stopped by to thank Korey and me for performing— and tell us the fair had already raised enough money for the food bank! We couldn't have ended the night on a better note.

Who knew my friends and I would work better by splitting apart? Don't get it twisted, I still loved when we came together and crushed it, but I guess "together" could mean different things. And after this night, I couldn't wait to see what my girls and I would do next!

Rhiannon Richardson writes and edits content for children and young adults. She is a proud advocate for marginalized voices in literature and uses vibrant storytelling to expand the worldview of readers. She holds a bachelor's degree in English and creative writing from the University of Pittsburgh and lives in Philadelphia with her family and two guinea pigs, Moose and Bear.